For the Piermont Library Kids!!!

HAPPY DOG SIZZLES!

LISA GRUBB

PHILOMEL BOOKS • NEW YORK

"LISA GRUBB"

Published simultaneously in Canada.
Manufactured in China by South China Printing Co. Ltd.
Design by Deirdre I. Newman and Gina DiMassi.
Text set in 18-point Badger Medium.
The art for this book was created with acrylic paint on canvas.
Library of Congress Cataloging-in-Publication Data
Grubb, Lisa.   Happy Dog sizzles! / Lisa Grubb.   p. cm.
Summary: When the weather is too hot for Happy Dog and his friends,
they enter a contest to build the best walla-pa-doo—
a creation made out of junk—and wind up discovering
a way to cool off in the process.
[1. Dogs—Fiction. 2. Summer—Fiction. 3. Imagination—Fiction.
4. Junk—Fiction. 5. Recycling (Waste)—Fiction. 6. Contests—Fiction.]
I. Title.   PZ7.G93184Har 2004
[E]—dc21   2003006311
ISBN 0-399-24193-0
1 3 5 7 9 10 8 6 4 2
First Impression

Dedicated to Billie,
may all her dreams and wishes come true.

And special thanks to Deborah,
the craziest walla-pa-doo ever!

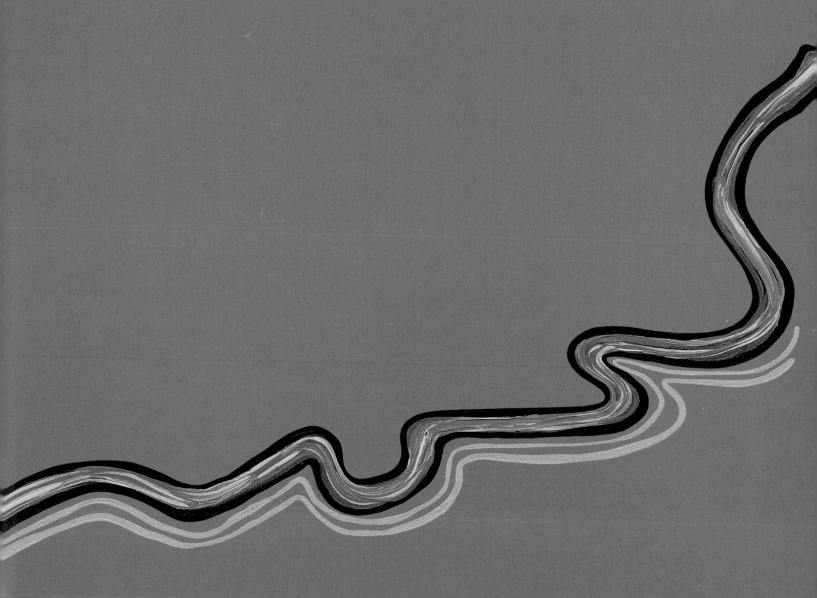

It was a hot summer day. The blazing sun made everyone want to hide inside. Happy Dog and Jack Cat were bored.

"There must be something we can do to cool off," said Happy Dog.

"Let's go to the park," said Jack Cat.

"Maybe we can go swimming."

So Happy Dog and Jack Cat went to
the park, but the pool was too crowded!
"We'll never get cool at this rate,"
said Happy Dog.

Just then they saw Captain Corkey Pup putting up a big sign.

"What does it say?" asked Happy Dog.

"It says there will be a contest for the best walla-pa-doo," answered Jack Cat.

"That sounds like fun!" said Happy Dog. There was only one problem. Neither of them knew what a walla-pa-doo was!

"A walla-pa-doo is anything you make from your imagination," Captain Corkey Pup told them. "My junkyard gives out a blue ribbon for the best one. Come along and see if you can build something — but remember, it needs to be special."

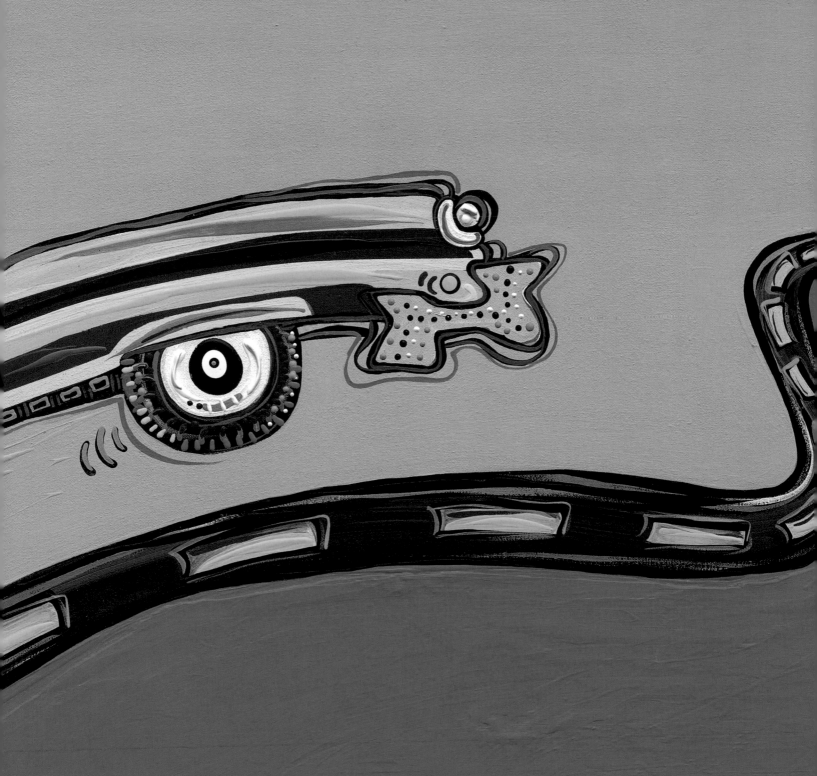

So they went to the junkyard with Captain Corkey
Pup. "You kids have fun!" he said when they arrived.
"I can't wait to win the contest!" said Jack Cat.

They looked around at the piles of junk.

"Here's a lamp that looks like a fish, and an old garden hose," said Jack Cat.

"I see an old tuba and a broken hat," said Happy

Dog. "Just think what great things we can build!"

So they built their first walla-pa-doo. But when they were finished, no one knew what it was they had built!

"Hmm," said Happy Dog. "It *looks* special, but what can it do? We'll have to do better than this if we want to win that contest. Let's look for more junk."

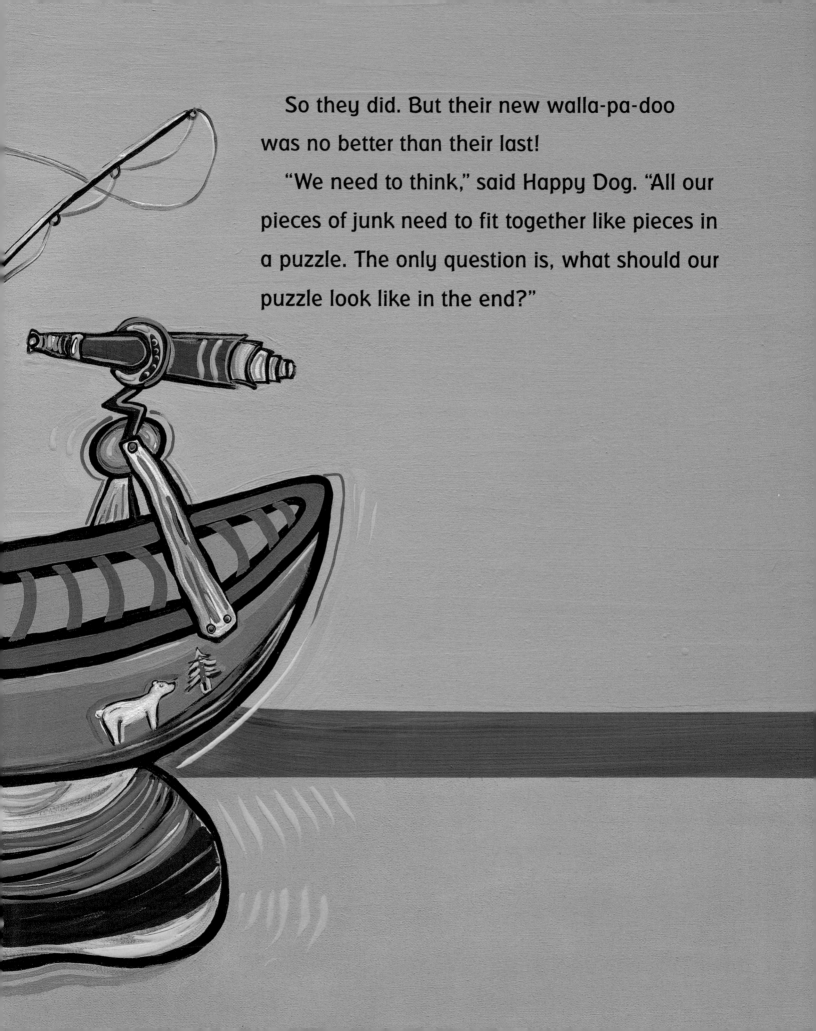

So they did. But their new walla-pa-doo was no better than their last!

"We need to think," said Happy Dog. "All our pieces of junk need to fit together like pieces in a puzzle. The only question is, what should our puzzle look like in the end?"

So they sat and thought. . . .

When that didn't work, they walked around and thought. . . .

When that didn't work, they danced around and thought.
"It's too hot to think this hard!" said Jack Cat. "I wish we had something to cool us off."

"That's it!" said Happy Dog. "Let's build something to cool us off!
That's what our puzzle will be."

"Why don't we just hook up the old garden hose and spray each other?" asked Jack Cat.

"Because that wouldn't be a very special walla-pa-doo," answered Happy Dog. "We want to win the contest, remember?"

So they collected more junk, only this time they knew what to look for. Happy Dog found a broken drum and Jack Cat found an old suit of armor.

Then Happy Dog took the tuba he had found earlier . . .

And Jack Cat brought over the fish lamp . . .

"Now watch this!" said Happy Dog,
attaching the garden hose to the spigot.

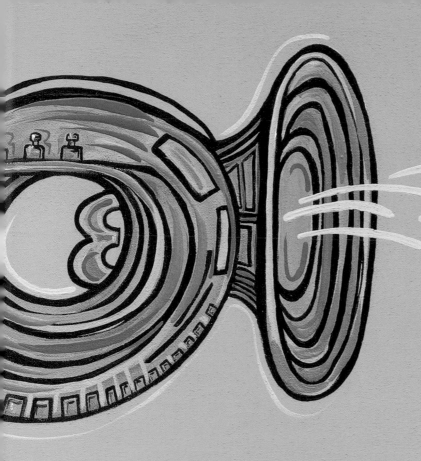

It was the most wonderful sprinkler ever!

"We did it!" said Happy Dog. "We built a great walla-pa-doo. We'll win that contest for sure."

"Who cares about the contest?" said Jack Cat as he ran through the water. "I'd say we already won."